The Sweet Smells of Zahramay Falls

By **Mary Tillworth**
Illustrated by **Cartobaleno**

Random House New York

© 2018 Viacom International Inc. All rights reserved. Published in the United States by Random House Children's Books, a division of Penguin Random House LLC, 1745 Broadway, New York, NY 10019, and in Canada by Penguin Random House Canada Limited, Toronto. Random House and the colophon are registered trademarks of Penguin Random House LLC. Nickelodeon, Nick Jr., Shimmer and Shine, and all related titles, logos, and characters are trademarks of Viacom International Inc.
rhcbooks.com
ISBN 978-1-5247-7277-2
MANUFACTURED IN CHINA
10 9 8 7 6 5 4 3 2 1

It was a beautiful day in Zahramay Falls.
"I have an idea," Leah said to Shimmer and Shine.
"Let's have a picnic!"

The friends went to the bazaar to find some yummy treats. First, they got delicious lemonade and mint tea to drink.

Next, they went to the vegetable stand to buy cucumbers and tomatoes.

At the bakery stand, they picked out a fluffy loaf of bread. Now they could make sandwiches!

The friends also wanted a zazzleberry pie—but the bakery was sold out!

Leah had another idea. She went to the fruit stand and bought some zazzleberries.

Then she got a cinnamon stick at the spice stand.

Finally, Leah bought eggs, butter, flour, and vanilla beans at the grocery stand.

With a little magic, the genies put all the ingredients together.

"*Boom, Zahramay! Shimmer and Shine, zazzleberry pie divine!*" they said.

Zac and Kaz joined Leah and the genies. Zac showed off his latest invention: pizza pancakes!

Zeta and Nazboo were out shopping for potions
when they saw Leah and her friends in the bazaar.
"Yum—pie!" Nazboo exclaimed.
Leah smiled and invited them to the picnic.

"A picnic? With genies?" Zeta exclaimed. "Ugh, fine. But just for you, Nazboo. I don't need any of that scrumptious zazzleberry pie!"

The friends found a grassy spot and spread out a blanket for a fabulous feast. Everyone had a great time . . . even Zeta!

What a magical, *scent*-sational day!